Beeper wears a silly hat.

Stomp laughs.

Beeper wears a silly coat.

Ha!
Ha!
Ha!

Stomp laughs.

Beeper wears silly shoes.

Stomp laughs.

Beeper gives Stomp a present.

Beeper and Stomp laugh and laugh.

Beeper walks to Honk's house.

Honk is not at home.

Beeper walks to Winky's house.

Winky is not at home.

Beeper walks to Stomp's house.

Stomp is not at home.

Beeper walks to his own house.

"Surprise!"

Honk and Beeper drive bumper cars.

Honk bumps Beeper.

Beeper bumps Honk.

Bump

Honk bumps Beeper again.

Beeper bumps Honk again.

"Honk honk!" says Honk.

"Beep beep!" says Beeper.

"Bump me again!" they shout.

Beeper plays music for Winky.

The music sounds bad.

Beeper plays more music for Winky.

The music sounds bad.

Winky plays music for Beeper.

The music sounds bad.

Beeper and Winky play music.

The music sounds great.